# Lucy Lombos

# Cotton and Nibbles

# Illustrated by Nisansala Alwis

This is a Children's Book, published by Lombosco Publications, Canada.

Date Published: **June 30, 2021**

# Dedication

This children's book is dedicated-

*To my Little Cherubim,*

*Grow in God's wisdom, greatness and loving stature.*

# Lucy Lombos

# Cotton and Nibbles

## Illustrated by Nisansala Alwis

"Hey, are you chewing on that page?" a young rabbit asked.

"Oh, I'm sorry!" a startled tiny mouse replied.

"Books are so important!"

"But...I'm so hungry."

"Well, books from this library bin are not for snack time."

"A small bite will satisfy my tummy."

"But you're nipping it. Books are considered treasures," explained the bunny, as he wiggled his nose.

"I apologize," the mouse became so meek.

"I can give you nuts. Just don't nibble at the books," the young rabbit calmed himself, "What is your name? I am Cotton."

"Oh, hello! I'm Nibbles. I live inside the church... Nuts? Yes, please."

"Nice meeting you, Nibbles. Let's get out of here."

Cotton and Nibbles started to feel at ease with each other.

"I'm from Coneylandia," Cotton said as they crossed the street.

"You live at the back of the church, then," Nibbles replied.

"Yes, that makes us neighbors."

"Why were you at the book bin?" asked Nibbles.

"I love books! I want to learn the meaning of Easter," Cotton reasoned out.

"Wow, learning is good! I have heard the priest explains its meaning."

"So you know something about it?" Cotton asked in a curious tone.

"Remember, I am a church mouse! One of the walls has a small hole. That's my home," Nibbles shared. "So, when the priest talks, I get to listen. Come, follow me! I can show you the meaning of Easter."

"Oh, I thought we're going to read about it. Sorry, but because Easter is fast approaching, I really want to understand it. It's coming in five days!"

"Don't worry, Cotton. You will start to understand it really fast."

4

Nibbles was about to explain further, when Cotton's big family showed up. They came with nuts and fruits, and gave some to Nibbles.

"Oh, lots of food for a big family! See, Cotton, you and your siblings are all Easter bunnies."

"Why are we Easter Bunnies?"

"I'll tell you why. Let me eat first,"Nibbles said with a wink.

"Your parents give birth to a litter of bunnies like you with a fluffy, cotton-like tail and long, straight up ears."

Yes, but how is that related to Easter?" Cotton was yearning for more.

"Well, you, bunnies are known to produce so many offspring," Nibbles said, swallowed a crunchy nut and continued, "Since bunnies are born every few months, you have become a symbol of new life!"

"Now I am seeing the meaningful connection, "Cotton said and nodded his head.

The next day, Cotton visited Nibbles in his hole. She brought slices of cheese to Nibbles.

"Hmmm... yummy! Thank you for bringing me some cheese!"

"Four more days before Easter!"

"Exactly! Come along, I will show you more," Nibbles said after eating his last piece of cheese.

"Lovely garden!" Cotton exclaimed as they passed by some flowers.

"These are Easter lilies. In winter, they seem dead."

"Ah, since it's spring, they are now blooming."

"Indeed, they are reborn, blossoming and giving glory to its Maker!"

"Just in time for Easter, right, Nibbles?"

"You are correct, Cotton!"

"Let's go farther at the church's backyard," Nibbles invited his friend.

"What can we see there? Cotton asked.

"You'll be surprised. Be patient."

They stopped after a short walk.

"Can you see the chicken coop?" Nibbles asked.

"Oh yes, I think mother hens are hatching their eggs. Is that another meaning of Easter?"

"Yes, hens hatch their eggs to bring out new life in the same way as Jesus was risen!"

"Wow, that makes a lot of sense!" Cotton's eyes grew wide in awe.

Three days before Easter, Cotton brought a piece of banana for Nibbles. In return, Nibbles brought Cotton to the church's altar.

"Today is Good Friday. The cross is coverred with a purple cloth."

"Why?" a confused Cotton inquired.

"That's Jesus! He died on the cross to free us from our sins."

"That's the greatest love I've ever heard of."

Nibbles went on, "That's true! On Easter Sunday, He will rise again from the dead. The purple covering will be removed."

"You mean He will come back to life?" Cotton asked.

"Correct, that's what I have learned from the priest. Now, do you understand the meaning of Easter?"

"It's clear to me now! I can understand that Easter means the newness of life."

"I'm glad you got it!" Nibbles was excited for his new friend.

"Thank you, clever mouse, for teaching me!" Cotton was so grateful.

"You're welcome! Come by again."

"I'd love to, but I would join my family in packing the Easter goodies."

"I see! That means you will be very busy. Enjoy the tradition!"

Easter has come! Those who believe in Easter are joyful of the celebration.

It was still early, but Cotton has started giving away some Easter baskets. Then, he went to look for Nibbles at the church.

"Hi, Nibbles! I brought you something!"

"Wow! Goodies!" Nibbles got very excited.

"Inside the basket are painted eggs. Remember they are one of the symbols of Easter? Well, there are some sweets, too."

"Thank you for this special treat, just as Easter is a perfect gift for the believers!" Nibbles uttered. Then, he noticed something in Cotton's hands. "Why do you have Easter lilies?"

Before Cotton could answer, the church bells rang.

"Happy Easter, Nibbles!"

"A joyful Easter to you, Cotton!"

"These Easter lilies are for the church altar!" Cotton said and went on his way.

The priest was getting ready for the holy mass. As soon as he stood at the altar, he saw an Easter bunny.

Cotton ran around the priest's feet in circles, while holding the lilies.

The priest couldn't help but smile. He gently picked up Cotton and said, "Your flowers capture the sacred spirit of Easter."

Cotton twitched his nose and nudged the priest, as if to say "Yes, new life!"

From afar, Nibbles looked on and whispered, "You nailed it, my Easter bunny!"

- The End-

## SPECIAL REQUEST

To all those who bought and read this book-

If you loved this Children's Book and have a minute to spare, the author would really appreciate a short review from you to be posted on the site where you bought or read the book. Your help in spreading kind words is a great succor to other readers, especially to the young children from different parts of the world.

## GREAT THANKS!

# *** The Author ***

Hi! **Lucy E. Lombos** is the author of this Children's Book.
Each letter of her first name has meaning.

**L- Light**. Yes, that's right, the bubbly light of the family! She is a loving daughter and sister, a wife, a mom of three sweethopes, a jolly friend and a brilliant teacher. She always asks the Holy Spirit to enlighten her mind, to inspire her and guide her all the time. Praise God! Modesty aside, she graduated with Honours- Valedictorian in Elementary, Silver Medallist with General Excellence Award in High School and Cum Laude in College. In De La Salle University, Taft, Manila, she pursued her graduate studies; and completed the academic units at the University of the Philippines where she specialized in Language and Literacy. She further enhanced her English proficiency skills by enrolling in a TESOL (Teaching English to Speakers of Other Languages) with Practicum Course in Vancouver, British Columbia, Canada.

**U- Understanding**. She has a substantial and deep understanding of her profession. She undertakes teaching the English fundamental skills, and these are – Speaking, Reading, Writing and Listening. She founded Lombosco Academy in the Philippines in 2000 and she remains the Academy Directress, and the Editor-In-Chief of its Newsletter.

**C- Children.** They are the subject of her craft. She studied courses about Writing for Children, Writing a Life Story, and Writing Young Adult Novel in Canada. She also earned a Diploma in Child Psychology in USA. In Spring time of 2020, she enrolled in Child Protection: Children's Rights in Theory and Practice at the Harvard University edX.

**Y- Young.** She is always young at heart. She would like to learn more. She never stops resting on her laurels. She enjoys blogging and contributing articles for different media. Further, she is a member of ILA- International Literacy Association and Society of Children's Book Writers and Illustrators.

*N.B. *In the Philippines, Lucy taught at Puerto Galera Academy after her College Graduation; later, she became the Principal at Prince of Peace Montessori. *Through her authored books, in 2017, Puerto Galera's Sangguniang Bayan gave her an Official Recognition for promoting tourism in that province; In October 2019, another Special Recognition was awarded to her by the Puerto Galera Tourism Council. *She always gives and donates FREE Books, and she says, "It's my wish that my books would find their way to all young readers' hands and hearts."*

# *** ACKNOWLEDGMENT ***

I would like to express my deep gratitude to the following people for giving me the big support which I humbly needed in writing this book –

Umberto Lombos for publishing this book;

Annie Datu-Enriquez for editing the manuscript;

Ely, my mom and the entire Enriquez family for supporting me morally;

Marianne Maristela,

Je-an Villamor,

And

Emily Yu

for writing the beautiful blurbs for this book.

I am truly happy and grateful to you all.

# The Major Sponsors

## LOMBOSCO ACADEMY FOUNDATION, INC.

### Since 2000

**Telephone numbers: 8842-7992; 8842-6519**

**Address:**

**# 11 C. Arellano St/, Phase 1, Katarungan Village,**

**Poblacion, Muntinlupa City, Metro Manila.**

## MAGNIFICAN IMMIGRATION AGENCY

**Website: magnificanimmigration.com**

## *** Her Other Published Books are***

*Ang Tinago Kong Piso/The Peso-Coin I Kept*

*The Class Lady Bug*

*The Star of the Sea: A Boat Ride*

*Happiness 365 and ¼ Days (a biography)*

*'Ter and Ter', the Turtle and the Eagle*

*The Joys of Junior*

*Swanie's Bag*

*Rose of Calapan (a novel)*

*Bono (an early chapter book)*

*Three Fables, Part 1: Keys to Change the Heart,*

*Three Fables, Part 2: Sparks to Brighten one's Purpose in Life*

*Pinky Oinky*

*Gracie and Dots*

*Noshi*

*One Drop, Two Drops and Much More*

*Ellie-Phant and Mon-Keysha*

*Ely's Gift*

*Monsters in Lazareto*

## *** Her upcoming books are- ***

Beary G

Love, Fishbeak

and

*The Seed*